I wish, I wish
With all my heart
To fly with dragons
In a land apart.

By Irene Trimble

Illustrated by The Thompson Brothers

Based on the characters by Ron Rodecker

Text and illustrations copyright © 2004 Sesame Workshop. "Dragon Tales" logo and characters ™ & © 2004 Sesame Workshop/Columbia TriStar Television Distribution. All rights reserved.

Visit Dragon Tales on the Web at www.dragontales.com

Watch us on PBS!

One rainy day, Emmy was busy tidying up the playroom while Max poked around in his toy box for something to play with. "Want to help me work on a puzzle?" Max asked as Emmy began dusting the shelves.

"I can't," she told him. "I haven't finished my chores yet."
Emmy watched as Max placed the puzzle on the table. "Hey,
Max," she said, "how did you get *your* chores done so fast?"

Max gave her a big smile and lifted up the corner of the carpet. "Easy!" he said. "I found a shortcut! I swept all the dust under the rug and piled all my stuff in the closet!"

When Emmy opened the closet door, all of Max's toys came tumbling out.

Luckily for Max, at that moment the magic dragon scale in their window seat suddenly began to glow. "Yay!" cried Max as he and Emmy held the shimmering dragon scale. "Let's go to Dragon Land! I'll clean it up later!"

Max and Emmy swirled out of their playroom and into the magical world of Dragon Land.

"But where are the dragons?" asked Emmy, looking around. She looked up and saw dragons of every size and color flying across the sky.

"I wonder where everyone's going!" exclaimed Max. "Maybe the sign on that tree can tell us. Can you read it, Emmy?"

Emmy had just begun to sound out the words when the tree suddenly leaned over and said, "Let me read it for you!"

Max and Emmy laughed as the gnarled tree put on its glasses, cleared its throat, and peered down to read the words written on the sign.

"Attention, all dragons and friends of dragons! There will be a giant fireworks display in the Whispering Woods Stadium TODAY! Just take a map and watch for the signs!"

The old tree handed Max and Emmy a map drawn on one of its large green leaves. They thanked the tree and headed off.

The children looked at the map carefully. "Gee," said Emmy. "It sure looks like a long way to the Whispering Woods Stadium."

"Maybe we don't have to walk the whole way," said Max, spotting a knuckerhole ahead. "We could take a shortcut! If we jump down the knuckerhole like Zak and Wheezie, I bet it will take us there!"

"Great idea!" agreed Emmy as she and Max peered into the knuckerhole. "We could get there in no time! Let's do it!" And they jumped into the knuckerhole together.

"This is almost as much fun as flying!" yelled Max.
He and Emmy slid down and around the curves of the
glittering knuckerhole. But instead of ending up at the
stadium, they tumbled to a stop right in front of Zak
and Wheezie's cave.

"Zak? Wheezie? Anybody home?" asked the children as they looked for their favorite two-headed dragon. But Zak and Wheezie were nowhere in sight.

"Now what?" said Emmy, looking at all the other tunnels. "We don't know where any of these tunnels go."

"I guess we're going to miss the fireworks," sighed Max as he and Emmy sat down on the floor.

But just then, a little light flashed on the wall of the tunnel. Then another . . . and another! Soon the air was twinkling with colorful lights.

"Are these the fireworks?" gasped Max.

"No," answered a hundred tiny voices. "We're glitterbugs. Our job is to stay and light the way."

Max and Emmy explained that they had been trying to take a shortcut to the stadium. "But now we don't know how we'll ever get there," said Emmy.

"Well," flashed the little glitterbugs, "sometimes shortcuts aren't shorter, and the long way isn't as long as it seems."

Max thought about how he'd swept the dust under the playroom rug. He'd have to go home and do his chores all over again! "Yup," said Max. "That's how it can turn out, all right. Our trip to the stadium will take even longer now!"

"Don't worry," the glitterbugs told them. "We can make fireworks, too!" Max and Emmy were dazzled as their tiny friends lit up the walls of the knuckerhole in rainbows and bursts of light.

As Max and Emmy watched the light show, they suddenly heard loud voices coming from up above them.

"I just want to drop off my sun hat," said one voice.

"I told you you wouldn't need it," said the other voice. "Fireworks only happen at night."

"Well, you never know."

Max and Emmy recognized the voices in an instant. It was Zak and Wheezie!

"Max! Emmy!" shouted Zak and Wheezie when they spotted their friends down below. "Why aren't you watching the fireworks?"

Max and Emmy explained what had happened when they'd jumped down the knuckerhole.

"Looove it!" cried Wheezie, clapping her hands for the glitterbugs. "But the fireworks haven't started yet, so why don't you come back with us?"

"Hurry!" the little glitterbugs told them. "Don't miss the show!"

Max and Emmy thanked the
little glitterbugs. Then they climbed
on Zak and Wheezie's back.

As they flew out of the knuckerhole, the little glitterbugs flashed, "You're welcome!"

As Max and Emmy flew into the Whispering Woods
Stadium, Ord ran up to give them a giant hug.
"We are so happy to see you, *niños*!" said Quetzal as
he handed them dragon sparklers.
"You're just in time!" Ord exclaimed.

Beautiful bursts of fireworks filled the sky. Everyone oohed and aahed. Ord lifted Max onto his shoulders so he could see better. It was a wonderful show!

Max and Emmy returned to their playroom still talking
about the two amazing light shows they'd seen in Dragon Land.
Max knew what he had to do next. He lifted up the rug,
then chased the dust bunnies into a dustpan.

"Gotcha!" Max said.

"Nice work, Max!" giggled Emmy. "If the glitterbugs could
see you, they'd say, 'Good job!'—in a twinkle!"